THE FEAST OF DEAD MAN'S HOLLOW

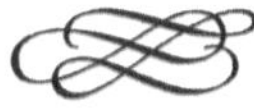

DESIRÉE M. NICCOLI

For Jenny

CONTENT INFORMATION

You should always feel confident and safe when reading a book. As such, I've included a list of content information. If you have any concerns about the contents of this book, please be sure to check this list first.

This book contains sexual content. It is not intended for anyone under the legal age of adulthood. All characters depicted in sexual situations herein are over 18 years of age.

Other sensitive content within this book includes, but is not limited to: blood, death, distress and grief, life threatening situations, near drowning, attempted murder, murder. But no graphic descriptions.

CHAPTER 1

Something in the bog was watching. Theodore felt the unseen eyes as he picked his way across sodden ground, cutting a familiar path toward a solid strip of land where trees still grew. Something always watched within Dead Man's Hollow. Never anything he could see, but whether it was the birds or some other creature, he never gave it too much thought. Today, however, the fine hairs at the nape of his neck prickled as he scanned the trees for hidden security cameras, his heart a jackhammer inside his chest, chiseling away at flimsy courage.

It wasn't like Theodore to risk his neck.

But he'd do anything for this bog, including keeping it untouched by those who thought that the best way to appreciate beauty was to build a resort on it.

Fog rolled off standing water, curling its wispy tendrils around the leatherleaf and stunted black spruce that jutted from vibrant red mats of sphagnum moss.

He sloshed through a partially submerged area in his waders, using a walking stick to test the bottom. It was soft but holding firm, enough to hold his weight, at least. As he trudged, wafts of slowly rotting peat—all at once earthy, dank, and slightly floral—plumed the air.

There was a cluster of sundews ahead, their brightly colored rosettes tipped with dewy, sticky filaments, sweet to taste but designed to hold on and never let go. Each tiny maul secreted a digestive enzyme that broke down the plant's trapped prey and absorbed it.

Bending to examine the carnivorous plant, Theodore was mildly disappointed to see it hadn't caught anything in its embrace, its stems still unfurled and reaching. But it was only a matter of time before an unlucky insect fell for its dangerous welcome.

To have and to hold.

To hold and to feed.

Theodore had always loved the pretty, vicious things.

Climbing from the murk and onto firmer ground, he entered the copse of trees, each step squelching. A lone, dead larch towered before him. Its trunk was as smooth as bone, bleached white by sun and time, every one of its branches bare and broken. Near its base was a hollow, an opening in the trunk just large enough for a child to squeeze into. He knew, because once upon a time, it had been his favorite hideaway. The place he returned to again and again to read or draw or daydream until the sun hung low in the sky.

Dead Man's Hollow was a dangerous place to explore. Its many hazards were fodder for grisly tales—of people getting lost in the fog and swallowed by sucking mud, never to be seen again, of murder and ghosts and eerily well-preserved bodies dredged up from the murk. But Theodore always had a sixth sense for firmer ground, and he never found a body. Not a human one at least.

The peatlands he knew were rich with blueberry and cranberry patches; the former he ate by the handful, the latter collected for recipes. Sometimes he caught and released frogs or found a fallen log to sprawl across, basking in the sun. Often, he brought a book or notepad for sketching his naturalist drawings—dragging his mechanical pencil across paper to make little studies of the plants and wildlife he saw.

When he was a boy, his mother taught him how to safely walk the peat bog, how to appreciate its beauty while also respecting its dangers. She raised him in a solitary cottage at the bog's edge, its timber walls and river rock foundation holding the fond memories of his childhood, but since she moved into town to be closer to friends, it was all his own.

No one else dared venture inside Dead Man's Hollow, so it was a quiet place, *his place*, all to himself.

Or it was.

Theodore stared down the mud-splattered ditcher parked on a solid stretch of ground, unguarded but ready to dig the trenches that would drain the bog dry. To make the land "optimal for development."

All so big-tech billionaire Leon Marks could dabble in real estate and build a secluded lodge for the ultra-rich deep in the Maine wilds —accessible by small chopper only, an exclusive experience. What was good enough for the Rockefellers and Vanderbilts on Mount Desert Island wasn't good enough for Marks. He had to pillage precious, untouched land farther north.

All the town hall meetings Theodore attended, all the letters he wrote about the bog's ecological importance, none of it had mattered. The Town Council still greenlit the project, permits swiftly granted. When the construction crews came, shattering the peaceful quiet with their shouting and heavy machinery, Theodore knew he needed to be braver than he ever had before.

He was always so careful and safe in his explorations. Even with three decades of peatland familiarity under his belt, a network of firm ground vividly mapped out in his mind, he still carried a long stick equal to his height to perform depth tests. Poking here, poking there, but never quite stepping a foot out of line.

And now Theodore was about to do something very stupid.

Kneeling next to the machine, he slipped off his backpack, filled with wrenches, cutters, and other tools. He spent the day studying online diagrams and equipment manuals, learning how to best break a ditcher and delay development without hurting the bog itself. Then, he waited for the construction crew to pack up and leave for the evening.

What he called activism, others called sabotage. Or worse, eco-terrorism.

A cold sweat trickled down the back of his neck, and he paused to push a pair of glasses up the bridge of his nose. Black plastic frames that were usually paired with crisp button-down shirts and a compulsive need to iron his trousers. That is, when he wasn't wading through bog muck. While his sense of style, and his modestly gelled and side-combed hair, vibed better with the 1940s and 50s than 2025, he was no Clark Kent. More of a Fred Rogers in both personality and stature.

The most modern thing about Theodore's appearance was his smart watch and the tree line cuff inked around his right forearm. Nothing about his appearance made him feel confident enough to be any good at crime.

The fog thickened as he worked, hands stained with grime and grease. Overhead the sky darkened, and the temperature dropped, heralding a brewing storm—a storm his weather app hadn't warned him about today.

Every ghost story he ever heard crowded his thoughts—stories he ignored in the face of a beautiful, bountiful ecosystem. Shadows crept in, closing in from all sides, and when water splashed nearby, he nearly jumped out of his skin, certain cold, clammy, dead hands would seize him from below.

A creature's long, skinny legs kicked out, just beneath the surface, before disappearing into the murky water.

"A frog," he breathed, wiping away the cold sweat that broke out across his brow.

The nerves, the jumpiness, and the annoying armpit sweat, it was because he was doing something illegal. That's all. Not because there was anything haunted or supernatural to fear.

Leaving his walking stick behind, Theodore shuffled around the ditcher to better reach and mess with the engine. The sooner he got this done and over with, the better. But as he stepped down, wider than he meant to, the ground gave out beneath him, and he plunged backward into a pool of cold mud.

Panic made him flail and kick, thirty years of experience out the window in a single instance. The struggle made him sink deeper.

Stupid. Stupid. Stupid.

Overconfidence and complacency were deadly.

And Theodore had just made a fatal mistake.

CHAPTER 2

A horse whinnied.

Theodore's first thought was that if Leon Marks and his land development team caught him, he'd go to jail. The second was that he hoped they did and fished him out. His third thought was spent puzzling out why a billionaire would ride a horse into a bog. Sure, the filthy rich did all sorts of bizarre, eccentric things, but this was particularly strange and stupid.

Slowly turning his head, mud up to his ears, he was going to shout a warning, but instead watched with growing terror as a white, mud-splattered horse thundered toward him with impossible ease, as if there wasn't treacherous, sucking mud beneath its hooves.

And astride it was a woman clad in all black, from tattered long coat and riding leathers down to her gloves and boots. Her clothing was old, but not like the vintage styles Theodore wore. For all he knew, she could've been fresh off the set of a spooky period piece or a late 1700s reenactment, a renegade woman boldly decked out in what those times would consider men's clothing.

She was riding hard, her gaze pinned on him, dark brows pinched in fierce determination.

Just as he thought she'd blow past him, she withdrew her foot from the stirrup and slid bodily down the saddle in the most astounding feat of trick riding he'd ever seen in real life. Before he could process what was happening, she reached into the muck and grabbed him by the scruff of his collar, hoisting him out and into the saddle.

Next thing he knew, they were galloping out of the bog, weaving in and out between the trees, his rescuer perched snuggly behind him. Cool air whipped against wet skin, an unflattering recipe for chattering teeth and a runny nose. He eyed his shirtsleeve, covered in a thick layer of sludge, and sniffed back hard instead. That was the best he could do.

Too amazed by the circumstances to speak, he snuck a glance over his shoulder.

She had curly, raven-black hair cut chin-length on one side, undercut on the other, and brown eyes so dark they were nearly pools of black. Her skin tone could've rivaled moonlight, and if it was anything like his, no amount of sun exposure would tan it.

Unlike her roughened, old-timey clothing, her makeup seemed quite modern—smokey eyes and dark purple lipstick. The combination wouldn't be out of place in a Tim Burton movie.

Could there be camera crews nearby, filming in secret? Surely, he would've heard about a film production coming to the area.

But despite the impossibility, Theodore glanced back again, hoping to glimpse recognizable features.

A green ribbon was tied in a neat bow around her neck, a lovely pop of color offsetting her fiercely serious expression and grim attire.

He tried to parse her features further, considering if maybe he'd seen her on the cover of an entertainment magazine. But then his thoughts jumped to how much taller she sat in the saddle than him, how her broad shoulders and solid arms framed his body, and that perhaps she was the lady goth version of Henry Cavill instead.

He liked that. A lot.

With her arms pressed around him, holding the reins, and her leather-clad thighs squeezing his, radiating warmth he desperately wanted—no, *needed*—to soak in, he tried not to focus on every flex of muscle. Or how the horse's undulating motion rubbed their bodies together. The combination was wreaking havoc in places that made him grateful for his waders and being covered in cold mud.

Of all the things he could've said to this gorgeous woman, what came out of his mouth was a rambling stream of consciousness. "How'd you lift me up like that? I know there's not much to me, but one hundred and sixty pounds is still one hundred and sixty pounds. Is that even humanly possible?"

"Hmph."

His cheeks flamed with the force of a thousand suns.

Oh God, did he just insult her?

Not human, Ardruina thought. She kept that little tidbit to herself.

Her companion went beet red. "Sorry, that was rude. I didn't mean to imply that you couldn't lift me, or anything, that was just a seriously cool move. How'd you do that? Are you a power lifter?"

This shivering, mud-covered slip of a man was rather verbose for someone who just nearly died.

"Momentum." Ardruina leaned away sharply when he craned his head to meet her eyes, just barely avoiding a streak of mud across her chin. All that straining couldn't be good for his neck. Or hers.

The look he gave her was cutely skeptical. He was short enough that she could easily rest her chin on top of his head, and if it weren't for the mud, she might've done so, just to feel like she was the hero in one of those romantic fairytales. The kind she'd never star in.

Beneath the mud, she caught glimpses of light brown hair cropped short along the sides, and a longer section combed across the top and parted to the left. Very 1940s in style, if her memory served her. Blue eyes, square jaw. The barest hint of scruff.

"Well, however you did it, thank you for the rescue. Name's Theodore, by the way. Though you could call me Teddy for short."

She snorted. "I'm not calling you Teddy."

"Even though you're holding me like a …"

"Do not finish that sentence," she warned, though a smile threatened to overtake her face.

"… Teddy Bear."

"I can put you back where I found you."

"Sorry, I talk a lot when I'm nervous, and you're really pretty, which is no excuse for badly flirting, but I think almost dying is making it worse. Just ignore me. Or better yet, I'll shut up."

The words "pretty" and "flirting" danced circles in her head, rendering her speechless. Usually, people ran away from her screaming. They deserved it, but still.

"All my friends call me Theo, no one calls me Teddy, but I always thought it would be a rather cute endearment, you know?"

"Theodore?"

"Yes?"

"You're still talking." *Dammit.* That was meant to sound teasing, but it came out all wrong, even to her own ears.

He shrunk in on himself, cowed like a kicked puppy. While Ardruina wasn't by nature the benevolent sort, even she drew the line at puppy kicking.

This is why she hid herself away and left him alone all these years. Only watched from afar as he made his daily treks into the bog, a notebook in his breast pocket, a pencil tucked behind his ear. Why she never said a word while he talked to himself, playing out make-believe conversations with an infuriating botany colleague, even though she wanted to tell him he needed to stop being so forgiving and get the man fired.

Or best yet, when he smiled, cheeks made round and rosy from mirth, the day he sketched a little brown bat in a teacup and named it Buttons. She didn't know how so nonsensical a name could be that cute and charming. After all, what did buttons have to do with bats? But she never approached to ask, too afraid to wipe that smile from his face.

Sometimes, when she dared too close, he'd look up from his drawings to survey the landscape, sensing, squinting, searching, but never finding, before shaking his head and carrying on.

You couldn't catch something as elusive as mist.

And sometimes, when the ground was especially tricky or a bear and her cubs ventured near, she followed him home, making sure he made it there safely. She watched from afar, hidden amongst the trees, as he stomped up to his front stoop, knocking large chunks of muck from his boots. And she kept watching, much longer than needed, his routine becoming as familiar to her as the back of her hand. How he whisked open his screen door, and through that sheer material, observed him shuck off his waders and his mud splattered shirt, revealing a pale, slight frame.

Time had never helped her figure out what to say to him, prolonged solitude making her socially inept. This sweet, shy man didn't deserve to feel her conversational snarls, not when he'd been a friend and ally to the bog all his life. He even tried to protect it in his own clumsy way, and it nearly cost him his life.

She had to fix this, somehow.

"My name's Ardruina." It wasn't much of an olive branch, so she wrapped her cloak around him and pulled him closer, shielding him as much as she could from the chill, autumn air. The poor man had very little body fat, and his sodden clothes weren't doing him any favors. "Just Ardruina, though," she added, before he could get any clever ideas. "I don't like nicknames."

Theodore perked up right away, bringing his back flush with her chest. "Never heard that one before, but it's beautiful. Wouldn't dream of shortening it."

The way he sunk his weight into her arms just then, relaxed and perfectly at ease, seeking comfort—*no*, stability—she tightened her hold, because after today's clumsiness, wouldn't it be just her luck if Theodore fell off the horse, too.

Ardruina meant to leave him at the edge of the forest, where the wilds and his cottage met. Leave him so she could return to her solitude and distance, all secrets intact.

What need did she have for a companion when Dead Man's Hollow kept her in good company all these years?

Every morning, she watched the rising sun burn off the morning fog with its golden light; listened to the trees' greeting, their branches creaking and leaves rustling as they swayed with the wind, harmonized by birds and trilling frogs.

What more did she need when she lived in a place that brought her peace?

But then Theodore sniffled again, his body shaking like a leaf, despite her efforts to keep him warm. She couldn't leave him like this. Not in this state. Just as she'd done all those times before when something threatened his well-being, she had to make sure he was going to be okay.

With an encouraging kick to her mount's sides, she rode them deeper into the forest.

Kidnapping, but for a good cause.

CHAPTER 3

"Is this your home?" Theodore stared at a certifiable log cabin. Stone chimney and stacked log walls, it was the kind of old-timey, single-room structure you'd expect to see on the front of a maple syrup bottle. Or a Bob Ross painting.

The mysterious horsewoman named Ardruina nodded as she helped him out of the saddle, her leather-gloved hands enclosed around his waist, steadying him as he swung down. No sooner than his feet touched the ground did she let go, stepping away, and his chest twinged at the loss, a brief and silly spark of romantic hope smothered.

There was no reason for Ardruina to linger. No reason for Theodore to be disappointed by the newfound distance between them. And yet, without the steady feel of her, pressed up behind him, directing the horse with each flex of her sturdy legs, he felt two sizes too small in his own skin.

Then she met his eyes and smiled. It was all at once bright and reassuring, like she might be just as glad to have his company as he was to have hers. Warmth filled Theodore from the inside out, and just like that, everything fit again.

"We can go inside after we've washed up."

He swiped a hand down his front, a clump of mud falling away. "Good idea."

The horse would need tending to, but when he turned to help, it was gone.

"Um."

He scanned the trees, searching for its white hide in the fog, but the creature had vanished without a trace, quiet as a ghost. Not even hoofprints marked the dirt where it had stood.

Ardruina clapped a hand against his back. "Come on. Don't worry about Lady Crane. She'll return in the morning."

Strange. But if she wasn't worrying about the horse, neither would he.

Theodore followed Ardruina around the cabin to where there was a steaming hot spring and a small storage shack.

"Go ahead. Strip down and hop in. I'll bring soap and towels." Ardruina opened the shack door and disappeared inside.

The waders took the brunt of the mess, so by the time he peeled off all his layers, naked but for his glasses, he was just a shivering slip of cold, pale flesh, streaked with mud.

Casting nervous glances at the partially open door, he eased himself into the hot spring, feeling out the bottom with his feet. He couldn't help but exhale a sigh of relief as the heat seeped into his limbs. Cold bits shrinking up into his body? Not his best look. And not the first impression he wanted this gloriously jacked woman to have about his naked physique.

Setting his glasses aside, Theodore vigorously scrubbed mud off his face and out of his hair, wanting to look a little more presentable when Ardruina returned. For no other reason than he was wildly attracted to her, and if she bestowed upon him an ounce of attention, he'd die a happy man.

By the time Ardruina exited the shack, carrying a stack of towels and two bars of soap, he was lounging in the spring, arms spread wide, and only slightly squinting. Overall, he was going for cool but would settle on relaxed.

"Where's your glasses?"

He lifted them to his face, clear one moment, fogging the next. But in that split second, he noticed that the mud stains he left on her clothes were gone. She must've cleaned up while inside the shack.

"They don't do me a lot of good in here." He shrugged, affecting a carefree grin. *That sounded smooth, right?*

Nodding firmly, Ardruina strode toward him, and he jolted at her sudden, rapid approach, covering his junk with a startled splash. *Shit. Shit. Shit.* While the steam provided a little cover, the water itself was clear, and modesty prevailed over the cool bastard act.

A small smirk lifted the corner of her lips as she set a towel and soap bar beside him. She bent so close he could tilt her face and bring those plush, purple lips to his, if he dared to do such a thing. But dare, he didn't.

"Thank you." His voice came out a little breathless.

"Mind if I join you?"

He gulped, cupping himself tighter. Without his glasses, he wouldn't see much. That had to count for something. "I don't mind."

Everything would've been fine if she moved to the other side of the spring, but as brazen as a wood nymph, she yanked off her boots right beside him. Then her coat. Then her gloves. Then, oh God, her shirt and trousers.

Bare as can be, she slid in next to him, divested of everything except that pretty green bow around her neck. Tilting her head back with a soft moan, she asked, "Isn't this nice?"

He bit the inside of his cheek to keep his thoughts respectful. To not think about the sleek, rippling muscle and sheer power beside him. Or that she could crush his windpipe with a single hand, and he'd thank her for the privilege of her touch. "Mhmm."

Folding her arms behind her head, a motion that did nothing to obscure her chest, she cracked open one eye. "You have enough room over there?"

His cheeks were on fire, and dear God, he hoped she thought it was the steam. "Plenty." *Too much. Too little.*

"Good." She smiled and closed her eye. "We can go back for your tools in the morning if you want. Finish the job you started. Just thought you might want to rest."

After almost drowning in mud.

"You'd do that?"

"Protect the bog? Absolutely."

"What I'm doing is illegal."

She shrugged. "Draining the bog should be, too."

That was why delaying development was so important—to buy enough time for a key bill to pass that would block the project altogether. But once construction was further underway, it would be too little too late.

Peatlands like Dead Man's Hollow were essential terrestrial ecosystems, mitigating climate change and stabilizing the carbon cycle. Even though the known ones only covered about three percent of the world's land surface, they stored at least two times more carbon than all the standing forests combined.

Leon Marks could not, and would not, succeed. Not if Theodore could help it.

"I don't want to get you into trouble."

"You don't need to worry about that." Her tone was too serious to be a simple, reassuring platitude. When she said, "I'm the trouble that finds people," he believed her.

CHAPTER 4

Ever since Ardruina joined him in the hot spring, Theodore had been a constant shade of pink. And yet, at every opening she offered him to back out, to bathe separately, to ask for more space, he declined.

The sweet, shy man tried so hard not to look down, and mostly succeeded, but she could see that she was torturing him. And she brought him back here for a reason, hadn't she? Something more than just ensuring his general well-being, even if she didn't know it at the time.

The truth about Dead Man's Hollow, quiet sanctuary though it was, was that it highlighted loneliness, too. What was once a comfort, time had morphed into an ache.

When it came down to it, Ardruina had been starved of companionship and of touch for an ungodly amount of time, and Theodore seemed interested in both. A few centuries spent relentlessly haunting a remote stretch of forest, and making a sport out of scaring people away, was fun for a while, but it did her no favors in romance.

In hindsight, she'd maybe gotten a little too scary for her own good.

It would be nice to get lost in someone else for a little while.

Holding out a bar of soap, she asked, "Wash my back for me?"

"I don't know if that's a good idea." Theodore averted his gaze.

That gave her pause. She'd tease and he'd blush, but this was the first time he wouldn't meet her eye. "Is everything okay?"

He sunk deeper into the water, angling his body away from hers. "Um, yes, but I have an, uh, erection," he finally answered, wincing, as if admitting that cost him.

Maybe it had. Not only had his rosy color deepened, he also tensed. Either he feared her, or how she'd react to that knowledge.

"That doesn't bother me," she said gently. "But if it bothers you, I can leave, and meet you inside whenever you're ready to come in."

"Oh." He lost the frightened deer look. "It really doesn't bother you?"

She shook her head. "You said you thought I was pretty, and it's a natural reaction, right?"

"You are pretty. Really pretty, but I don't want to be a creep."

"You're not. I'm inviting you to touch me."

"Even with my…"

"Perhaps, especially."

"Oh." Surprise lit his features. "*Oh.*"

She winked.

He finally relaxed, taking the bar of soap from her outstretched palm. "All right. Turn around."

Fighting back a grin at her victory, she complied and listened to him work the soap into a lather.

Slick hands dragged up her arms, and as Theodore's ragged exhale tickled the base of her neck, her skin erupted in goosebumps. He was so warm at her back, close, but not quite touching his body to hers. Cupping one shoulder, he moved his other hand in tight, slow circles, massaging away her riding aches.

Scooping water into his palm, he trickled it down the length of her back, repeating the process over and over, before lathering his hands once more.

The smooth glide of his palms, the unhurried, savoring touch.

This. This was what she missed, what she needed. In indulging one aspect of herself, she neglected another. But no more.

His fingers skated along the base of her neck, and while light as a feather, they also teased the skin just below the ribbon, trekking too close to perilous ground.

She flinched. "Don't knock the ribbon loose," she warned. "Whatever you do."

Neither of them would like it if he did.

"I'll be careful," he promised.

Nipping the lobe of her ear with his teeth and a newfound daring, Theodore washed her front instead. He started with her belly, using tender, worshipping strokes. Wherever muscle dipped into valley, or succumbed to curve, his fingers lingered, dragging fragrant suds in their path. Then rinsed them away as he went. No inch of skin was left unexplored, and every pass of his hands brought contrasting sensations—comfort, relief, and a dizzying, desperate need for bolder, more intrepid touch.

She leaned into him. "Theodore, don't be shy."

"I'm not," he breathed. "Not with you." His hands drew up to cup and knead, all pretense that he was supposed to be washing her abandoned. "Is this good?" He pushed her breasts together, perfect handfuls, and he played careful mind to her nipples, plucking, and tweaking them into firm, purple peaks.

"Yes." She sighed, pleased but far from satisfied, and inched her fingers up her thighs, toward a rising ache. The temptation to touch herself beckoned. If she were alone, there'd be no denying that need, but denying herself Theodore's attentive fingers? That would be criminal. "Don't stop there."

Don't you dare.

He hesitated, the motions of his hands slowing but not completely stopping. "Tell me what you want."

To be her complete self. To not hold back for fear of scaring him.

To not be so damn lonely all the time.

She said none of these things. The desire pooling below her navel was safer than the one drawing a noose around her heart. "I want to ride your hand."

His breath hitched. "You do?"

"Desperately."

After one final squeeze, he released her breasts, laying his hands tentatively on her hips. She pushed her backside into his crotch, firmly acquainting it with his rigid length. "I think I'm in a dream. This is too good to be true."

Skies above, did he think she was toying with him? "Theodore," she growled, digging her fingers into the meat of her thighs. "Touch me."

He flinched behind her, perhaps startled by her impatience and gruff, demanding tone.

Dammit. If she didn't assume a gentler, more reassuring approach, she'd scare him off for certain. "Please?" she tried again, more softly this time. "I'd like it very much."

He reached around and…*Oh yes. Right there. Thank the stars.*

Nimble fingers coasted over the sensitive bundle of nerves bridging the apex of her thighs, applying the perfect amount of pressure, stealing her breath and curling her toes. "Like this?" he asked, a little unsure, but a whole lot of sweet.

"Yes. Just like that." Ardruina twisted, winding her fingers into his hair and claiming him in a brief, but heated kiss. Theodore's surprised gasp was quickly followed by a smile against her lips.

He split his attentions, working her clit with one hand, the other paying homage to her breasts, the motions of his hands bringing her body flush with his. Strumming, rubbing, setting her core ablaze.

Under his diligent care, she almost couldn't remember why she ever thought he was shy. All he needed was enthusiastic permission, and once he had it, he charged forward with exuberance.

"Feels so good," she praised, the words coming out breathy and fragile as she rocked into his hand. Things she never got to be.

Widening his stance, Theodore braced her in the cradle of his hips, and she sank her full weight into him, digging her fingers into his thighs as she quaked, drawn tighter than a bow. He stood firm, leveraging the hot spring wall to support her.

"I like pleasing you." He pressed a kiss to her shoulder, easing a finger inside, water sloshing as he worked his arm up and down. With each upward stroke he ground the heel of his hand against her, sending fresh jolts of pleasure racing up her spine. "But I don't know if I can make you come."

"Don't be modest. You know you can." Her voice was raw, needy. How could he not? She was nearly falling apart already, riding his palm.

"I don't." He nuzzled the groove between her shoulder blades. "Not a lot of practice. You may have noticed there's not much of me to look at..."

Fury sliced through her. Not at him. Never him.

She spun in his arms, tilting his head back by the chin to stare down into widening dark blue eyes. With her other hand, she hitched his leg between hers, right where she needed him. "Who told you that?"

"No one in particular." He lifted his shoulder in a halfhearted shrug. "I'm just small."

There was an old hurt lurking in his eyes. Whoever made him feel like he wasn't enough could go straight to hell. And they were damn lucky, too, that she hadn't been around to send them there.

She ran a thumb gently over his lower lip, wanting to steal every hurtful thing he might repeat about himself before he could say it. "You're perfect. And exactly who I want." And to prove it further, she eased into a rocking motion on his thigh, testing the feel of him beneath her, and watching his face closely as she did so. "Would I be doing this if I didn't want you?"

His lips parted on a shaky exhale. "No." His cheeks turned an adorable shade of pink, followed by a bashful smile.

"Can you do something for me, Theodore?"

"Anything."

"Show me how you touch yourself."

Blush deepening, he took himself in hand. Eyes blown wide. "Yes, ma'am."

There. That was the Theodore she wanted to see. A touch shy but utterly believing her desire.

His shoulder flexed as he stroked himself. She followed that trail of lean muscle, biceps to forearm, forearm to hand, hand to palm, grasped around needy, reddening flesh.

"That's it." She crooned, brushing back his hair, the lightly gelled waves now frizzy and undone by the hot spring's humidity. "Just like that."

And when she clasped her hand around his throat, applying light pressure, Theodore's leisurely pace kicked up a notch, water sloshing between them, as he gazed up at her with heavy-lidded eyes.

"You're so beautiful." The way he said it, one part declaration, one part awe, set her heart pounding, threatening to break free from the cage of her chest.

When she looked at herself in the mirror, it was only ever to check to see if her ribbon was secure. Everything else about her appearance just didn't matter. But now? Locked in Theodore's embrace? She wasn't immune to such admiration.

She slotted her lips over his, slowly savoring him, their tongues meeting in gentle caress. Earlier that day, she watched him pop a hardtack candy into his mouth, and now she tasted its lingering lemony sweetness. He felt so good and solid underneath her. It felt like a dream, but he was real. This was real.

A shared moan escaped between them, the rhythm of their bodies picking up speed, racing toward the precipice. When she drew back from the kiss, she tightened her hand around his throat, his pulse beating against her fingertips. A vein popped along his temple as his breathing became more ragged. "You're maddeningly handsome when you're disheveled."

"Maddeningly?"

She split her gaze between his hooded eyes, parted lips, and rapidly moving hand, growing wetter and hotter at the sight. "Seeing you like this, brings me close to the edge."

His throat bobbed against the palm of her hand as he swallowed.

Precum beaded at his tip, and Ardruina fixated on that point, eager to see him join her.

"Use me," he pleaded, and she did. She rode his leg with wild abandon, seeking, searching, until she found release upon the hard planes of his thigh, every muscle in her body drawing up tight as pleasure pulsed through her.

"Oh, fuck." His face contorted, and with another jerk of his hand, he spilled into the steaming water.

Their heaving chests rose and fell in tandem as her forehead fell to his, and she dropped her hand from his neck.

Ardruina wanted someone to share this bog with, but those sorts of commitments weren't made in the space of an afternoon, and secrets like hers didn't withstand the test of time. And yet, she didn't want what she started with Theodore to end here.

Maybe this could be a beginning, not an end.

It was foolish. Probably selfish, too, but she whispered it anyway. "I don't want to stop."

Theodore's nose brushed hers, nudging up her gaze, their eyes meeting. His gaze was so soft and giving. "Are you asking for more?"

He reached between them, coasting his fingers across sensitive flesh and sinking into her wet heat one by one. Her heart stuttered in her chest, all at once excited and relieved. He wasn't done with her. And she hadn't scared him away.

"Could we..." She tilted her hips, pressing into his hard flesh, still mercifully erect, letting her body do the asking.

"Don't be shy, Ardruina," he murmured, parroting her earlier words. "Tell me what you want." His fingers pumped in and out of her as his thumb rubbed circles.

She moaned. "Bury yourself in me."

"I am buried in you." The heel of his hand pressed harder into her to emphasize the point.

Her cheeks burned, and not just from the spring's heat. She gave him so many easy-ins and now he was demanding lewd confessions. His confidence was growing, and it thrilled her. *Wicked man.*

"It's okay." There was nothing cocksure about his tone. It was all gentle encouragement, as he rocked his hips. "You can say you want this."

"I do," she breathed. "I do want it."

The appendage in question twitched eagerly against her thigh. It hadn't slackened in the slightest.

"Just let me make sure I have a condom in my wallet."

He let go of her to reach back, dragging his pants over. Finding what he was looking for, he hopped out of the spring, sitting on the edge with his cock sprung proudly between them.

The man was slight, all modest, lean muscle—a body made for endurance, not power—but it did nothing to dim her desire. From afar, she watched his many long, careful walks through the bog, the way he yanked out invasive plants with a fierce dedication or crouched down to study sundews and pitcher plants with rapt fascination.

So many times, over so many years, she observed him, never once daring to leave the deep shadows between the trees. Too nervous to approach. Too afraid he'd see her for what she truly was. That is, until his life was in danger, and she could hang back no longer. Stuck in bog mud, there was nowhere for him to run, and she could not watch him die. That's all it took to break her tenuous restraint.

She pressed the palm of her hand to Theodore's cheek, and he leaned into the touch a moment before placing a kiss to her inner wrist. After some brazen posturing and a little bit of charm, she somehow convinced this man to fuck her.

Was it fair that she knew more about him than he did of her?

Twice, he sensed that something was off. First, with her strength. And second, with Lady Crane's abrupt disappearance.

She brushed off his questions so far, but for how long would that last? She didn't want to lie to him, not even by omission. But what other choice did she have?

Theodore rinsed his hands, darting a glance her way. Whatever he saw in her expression seemed to sober him, a little shyness creeping back in. "You rethinking this?"

"No," she said quickly, smoothing her hands over his thighs, before disappointment or self-doubt set in. Maybe not telling him the full truth just now made her a villain, but she was so used to being one, and she didn't really need to spill her darkest secret just to fuck a man, did she? "I want this. I want *you*."

"Good." He seized her in another kiss, mouth hungry and demanding. It was between these feverish kisses that he said, "I want you, too."

He was reassuring her, she realized. Affirming her feelings and making sure she knew this was okay. Caring for her even though this could be the one and only time for them. *Damn, this man was sweet.*

Theodore quickly sheathed himself, and she turned around, hearing rather than seeing him slide back into the water, getting into position.

They were really going to do this. Scratch this mutual itch together. She'd be such a liar if she said she didn't hope for this outcome. When she brought him home, leaning into the ride, or when she undressed beside him, the message was clear. *If you're willing, I'm willing.*

And they both were, but the water wasn't making it easy. Cursed friction and not the good kind. The angle wasn't doing them any favors either. Making no progress, Arduina puffed out a frustrated laugh, and Theodore dropped his forehead to her upper back, shoulders shaking as he gripped her waist.

"This is an inauspicious start," he chuckled. "Maybe we should go inside?"

Thunder rumbled overhead, and the darkening sky that had threatened rain finally opened into a deluge. That, if not also their physical struggles, certainly decided things.

"Come on." Grabbing his hand, Arduina pulled him from the hot spring.

CHAPTER 5

They rushed inside, naked and laughing. Kicking the door behind him, Theodore backed his tall beauty against the wall, hands at her hips.

He'd been so afraid of making her uncomfortable, of being too greedy for touch. And yet, there wasn't an inch of him that she shied away from, didn't ask for under heavy, panting breaths. And God, did that make him want to rise to the occasion in every sense of the word.

Brushing away a rain-soaked curl that had fallen into her eyes, Theodore cupped her cheek and rose on the balls of his feet to kiss lips still perfectly, and miraculously purple, no matter how many times he sucked them into his mouth, so sweet and full like slices of plum. She moaned softly against his mouth.

He spread first her legs, then her folds with his fingers. Without water to interfere, she was perfectly wet for him, and he was able to ease himself in with steady rocking motions from his hips, sliding into the hilt without further hindrance. "Is this what you need?"

She sucked in a shaky breath, thick thighs quivering around him before settling onto his hips. "Yes."

He did his best to hold and support her, hands hooked under her legs, despite their size difference. Society had things to say about what it meant to be a man. Being smaller than the woman he was with wasn't one of its ideals, but he gave her his all, and hopefully that would make up for what he lacked in stature and strength. He was a bit self-conscious about it, yes, but it only enhanced his resolve to give her the pleasure she deserved.

Ardruina rose and fell, the deep cut of her muscles flexing in his hands.

Thrusting upward, he pressed his forehead to the space between her breasts and clavicles. Fucking hell, she felt so good, and that she draped an arm across his back and entangled her fingers in his hair, holding him to her, only encouraged him further.

Every needy sigh and hitched breath between them were music to his ears. And just because he was the shorter of the two didn't mean they didn't fit well together, their bodies notching in all the right places.

"This enough?" he breathed, working through the burn in his thighs, desperate to make her fall apart around him.

"More than. You feel so good, Theodore."

They were moving in sync, bodies pitching forward and back. Upward and downward. A happy, affirming squelching sound originated from between her legs, and she didn't seem to mind that what he was packing was on the smaller side of average. He began mentally reciting mathematical equations to keep himself from blowing his load again too soon, all while threading his fingers between them, to lavish her clit with attention. It didn't matter that he came already, outside in the spring. It really didn't. Being with Ardruina like this was drawing him to the brink again.

A delicious ache overtook his legs as he sped up his thrusts. He dug into that sensation. God, he'd fuck her right, even if his body gave out to do it.

"Theodore," she panted. "Theodore!"

Pleasure mounted. And sweet fuck, he wasn't going to last if she kept that up. Nothing made him want to come again more than Ardruina singing his praises. But he only had the one condom, something he added to his wallet when he re-entered the dating scene.

They'd have to make this last, because he sure as shit didn't know whether he'd have another chance to do this with her.

"Tell me what you need, Ardruina."

A flood of warmth pooled between them as she got wetter. "That," she said. "Keep talking to me."

He liked learning what she wanted. And maybe he was a fool to think that meant he'd get another opportunity to fuck her, but damn it, he was going to roll with that optimism. "You're a goddess. Like the warrior Athena," he said, punctuating each word with a deep thrust, while his fingers worked overtime on her clit. "If I could do this forever, I would, but you make a man want to come so hard he can't see straight."

"Really?"

He wasn't expecting the self-conscious breathlessness in her tone, so he drove in with a particularly unforgiving thrust, hoping it effectively illustrated his sheer hopeless need of her. "I've been doing advanced math in my head almost this entire time to keep myself from coming too soon."

Something between a laugh and a hearty moan erupted from Arduina's lips. "I'm that desirable?"

It was a completely unvarnished question, so he fired off some vulnerability of his own, because the last thing he wanted was her to feel less than perfect. "Fuck yeah, you are. And I so desperately hope to make you come again."

This time, when she said his name, her voice broke. She hunched all around him, then clenched, her pussy fluttering, and nothing, not even expert-level Calculus, could keep him from blowing.

He swore out loud, filling the condom.

When the blissful mental fog that enshrouded his mind finally dissipated, he said, "I'm sorry. That wasn't even respectably close to forever."

"Don't downplay this."

He rolled his forehead against her chest, reluctantly withdrawing from her slick, heated flesh. "Wouldn't dare." He should chuck the used condom, but goddamn, he needed a minute.

Snaking an arm around his waist, and holding him flush, Ardruina said, "I grabbed your glasses." She presented them in offering. "Thought you'd like to see."

"You were holding onto those this whole time?" Grinning, he accepted the frames, pushing them onto his face, saying not a single word about how badly smudged the lenses were. Or that he would've liked to have seen her orgasm in hi-definition.

"Wasn't thinking straight."

"Yeah?"

"Too handsome," she purred, leaning in for another kiss. A flash of green caught his eye.

"Wait, wait, wait!" He held her steady, and she stiffened, her hurt expression cleaving his heart.

He didn't know why she asked him to be careful around her green ribbon. Whether it was purely cosmetic, or sentimental, or hiding something she was self-conscious about, he promised to take care wherever it was concerned.

And right now, it was coming undone.

They must have jostled it loose in their romantic enthusiasm.

"Shh, easy sweetheart. Your pretty ribbon's unraveling. Want me to fix it?"

She froze, the first time he ever saw fear in her eyes. It took him a second to realize she wasn't even breathing.

"Sweetheart?"

A tear rolled down her cheek. He barely knew Ardruina, that was true, but in their short time together, she didn't strike him as the type to cry, much less let someone else see it. She didn't even try to wipe the tear away.

"Please," she whispered, barely twitching a muscle.

"I've got you," he soothed, and gently pulled the sides that would tighten the base knot first. Once that felt secure, he pinned it in place with a pinkie, looped one side, then the other, and tied them together snugly, but not so much that the fabric cut into her skin. "There, how's that?"

Touching a hand to her throat, she sucked in a relieved breath, and hugged him so tight, the air whooshed out of him. "Thank you."

He smoothed his hands over her back, mapping her topography, where every hard muscle met soft valley. "I'm sorry for the nickname. 'Sweetheart' kind of just came out."

"Don't be, you earned it." She tucked her face into the crook of his neck. "And besides, I think I actually like it."

Theodore didn't know what had just happened between them but setting the ribbon to rights was important to Ardruina. He didn't need to understand the finer points of her relief and gratitude to appreciate the weight of it.

CHAPTER 6

The horse, Lady Crane, was waiting for them outside the next morning, saddled and bridled, just as Ardruina had said, but it still shocked him to see the creature. His clothes, too, had been cleaned.

"How?

Ardruina's smile was sad as she helped him into the saddle. "I don't think you'd believe me if I told you." Her tattered, black long coat flared out behind her, the hem only a few inches from the ground. Within the fabric's folds, a metallic gleam drew his eye to the curved blade at her side—a sickle.

"What's this for?" he asked, pointing at the blade.

She swung up behind him, fitting them neatly together, and clicked her tongue, spurring the horse into a canter. "Bushwacking."

A simple, believable answer, but uneasiness prickled beneath his skin.

That morning, while he brought up food from her root cellar to fix them both breakfast, she donned her riding leathers again, the same ones he met her in. The way she layered and tucked and tied, it was like watching her put on armor. And it made him wonder why.

Considering how they took pleasure in each other's company and how Ardruina yanked him into bed after, tucking him tight against her body, where he stayed from dusk until dawn, he would've thought the intimacy they shared meant fewer walls and barriers.

He was probably getting ahead of himself.

Everything about Ardruina was a mystery.

Why she dressed the way she did and lived deep in the woods without modern conveniences and had a horse that was more ghost than domesticated animal. Why she spent five minutes checking the green ribbon in a mirror and had enough strength to pull a full-grown man out of sucking bog mud and seat him on the saddle of a moving horse. Why he never saw but had always felt her presence.

Too many unlikely and impossible things combined. Maybe he wouldn't believe her if she told him. Or maybe he already knew something preternatural was afoot. Something out of a fairytale or folklore. But he wasn't scared, just sated and happy and ready to save Dead Man's Hollow, because the sooner he did that, the sooner they could continue what they started.

Theodore was naturally curious. Years of visiting the bog, turning over rocks, picking up critters, nurtured that instinct. But preservation and conservation shaped him, too. Knowing when to leave something be. To not take what wasn't freely given.

"You don't have to tell me anything you don't want to," he said, threading his fingers through hers, the leather of her glove warm and soft. "But if you did tell me, you might be surprised by what I'm willing to believe."

She tilted his head back, kissing him slow and deep, and smoothed a hand under his shirt, across his belly. "I like you," she murmured against his lips.

He reached to cup her cheek. "And I like you."

CHAPTER 7

All of Theodore's tools were right where he left them. His walking stick, too.

But Lady Crane was sidestepping irritably, her ears laid flat. Theodore didn't know much about horses, but he knew enough to be worried. Something had her spooked.

"Something's wrong," Ardruina said, looping a protective arm around him.

A branch snapped behind them, and the horse reared, kicking out her front legs. The moment Theodore felt himself sliding, he squeezed his legs and clung to the saddle, Ardruina bracing around him. When they returned to the ground, Ardruina's sharp cry pierced his ear, her weight and warmth disappearing.

"Ardruina!" he yelled, twisting to see if she fell.

Rough hands yanked him off the saddle. He landed on the ground with a hard smack, pain blooming in his shoulder. Lady Crane reared again, and he rolled away to avoid her flailing hooves.

"Uh, uh, uh. Where do ya think you're going?" He was seized by the front of his shirt and dragged, mud and groundwater soaking the fabric, rocks scraping his skin.

The man above him was ridiculously muscled and wore a black T-shirt two sizes too small, mud-spattered jeans, and ass-kicking boots. Also, he was gruff, bearded, and had never seen moisturizer in his life.

Just as a broken branch cut a wicked, painful slice into his back, Theodore was hauled to his feet, arms jammed behind him. The force of it was very nearly enough to dislocate his shoulders, and a pained, breathless whimper rushed out of his lungs. He hated how a man such as this would see it as a sign of weakness.

Heart pounding a million miles a minute, he observed the scene before him, his brain trying to catch up and assess the mess they landed in.

Two other men with similar builds had also pinned Ardruina's arms, though they strained to contain her. She fought their combined grasp, eyes dark glittering pools of rage, too strong and fierce for either of them to handle alone.

Watching it all from the sidelines was Leon Marks. He looked just as douchey in his designer aviators and bougie hiking gear as he did in a bespoke suit on the cover of *Forbes*. The smug bastard was chewing gum with his mouth open, flashing a too-white smile.

"Got us here two meddling weirdos playing at eco-warriors." Marks laughed.

"Let her go," Theodore demanded. "She's got nothing to do with this."

"You rode in together." Marks gestured blandly to Lady Crane, the agitated horse snorting and stamping her hooves. "Looks like aiding and abetting to me." To his goons, he added, "Get rid of him first, then his goth girlfriend."

"Get your hands off her!" Theodore thrashed. The man had an iron grip.

A fist collided into the side of his face.

"Theodore!"

It hurt, but not as much as it could've. And when he looked up, he saw Leon Marks dabbing at his knuckles with a tissue, which he then deposited on the ground with a careless flick of his fingers.

The asshole sucker-punched him.

As Theodore was dragged to the water's edge, a cold certainty washed over him. He knew what they intended to do. What they'd force Adrian to watch, what would befall her next.

Once shoved to the ground, he wrestled his arms free, clawing and punching. The goon had him by the shoulders, pushing him back and back and back, cool water lapping at his scalp. He was engaging in the hardest crunch of his life just trying to keep his head above water.

"Let him go, or I swear you'll regret this!" Ardruina shouted.

Marks ignored her, expression bored.

Adrenaline was on Theodore's side for now, but he couldn't break free, and he couldn't keep this up. The crash was coming.

If only he was stronger. If only he'd insisted on coming alone.

If only, if only.

Ardruina met his eyes then with a strange, distant calm. "I'm sorry, Teddy." With a rough yank, she freed one of her arms and ripped the green ribbon from her neck.

Her head tumbled to the ground. And her body with it, her shocked captors letting go.

Theodore screamed.

CHAPTER 8

Theodore clawed and thrashed and choked on water as Leon Marks's goon tried holding him down.

He didn't know how it was possible, to just lose one's head like that, but what mattered most, what hurt the most, was his Ardruina was dead.

Every nerve ending screeched agony, cried for blood and vengeance. If only he'd the strength to enact his will.

His captor's hold on him loosened just enough for Theodore to come up sputtering for breath. "What the fuck?"

Ardruina's head still lay on the ground, her face thankfully turned away. But her body sat up, and rose from damp earth, a gleaming sickle in hand.

What the fuck indeed.

There was no hesitation. She slashed right, and then left, lopping off the heads of the men who'd held her—one brutal stroke each—as if she was born to do it. Before they could even process what was happening. Before *Theodore* could process what was happening.

As if she'd done it before.

Chest squared, and arms tensed for more slashing, she cut a rage-fueled path along the ground. He didn't need the benefit of facial expression to know she was out for blood, and that the one holding him did not have long left to live in this world.

"Don't come any closer," the man stammered, pulling a knife from his boot. "Or I'll slit his throat."

Fuck that. Expending the last of his energy, Theodore grabbed the man's wrist with one hand and jammed the heel of the other into his nose, jerking his head back. Abdomen on fire and utterly spent, he collapsed, water rushing over his mouth and nose, gravity and the weight of the other man working against him.

A silver blade flashed overhead, all sound muffled as metal met flesh. Blood sprayed across the water's murky green surface, a streak of crimson just above his face.

The man, and his hulking weight, were wrenched away.

A headless, leather-clad figure came into view, visage distorted by a rippling, blood-speckled surface. It plunged a fist into the water and hoisted him up.

Theodore sucked in a great gulp of air. Whatever enabled this nature-defying feat, the timing was excellent for his screaming lungs, but maybe not his neck...

"It's still me, Teddy. Don't be afraid. You're safe now."

It was Ardruina's voice but thrown funny, as if she were twenty feet away and not right by his side, cradling him to her body. Her headless body. It made no damn sense, but he believed her.

An engine revved.

"Leon Marks's getting away," he croaked, pointing.

The asshole had an ATV.

After situating him somewhere solid and mostly dry, Ardruina stood and whirled around, her tattered coat sweeping out behind her. In one fluid motion, she mounted Lady Crane and raced after Marks.

Scrambling to his feet, Theodore followed on foot. He had to see, had to know.

Through the trees, he saw Ardruina riding down the fleeing billionaire. Arm raised high, she swung with vicious force, decapitating him in one blow from behind. Marks's head rolled and bounced to the side, fancy sunglasses flying. Without a living driver, the ATV crashed into a cluster of boulders with a sickening crunch.

As Ardruina circled back, riding at a steady gallop, sickle dripping blood, a voice behind him said, "I wanted to tell you, Teddy, but this is obviously a lot to confess."

He spun around.

Ardruina's fallen head, laying cheek down on a mat of pine needles, gazed up at him apologetically.

Shit. Damn. Fuckity. Fuck.

Get your act together, Theo, she needs you.

Breathe in. Breathe out.

"Are you okay?" he stammered, crouching down. Talking to an animated, decapitated head was not on his list of things to do today. "Do you have a concussion from the …?" He motioned the falling off part with his hand.

"It doesn't feel good, but I'm alive in my own way."

Right.

Her body reined in beside him and jumped down, retrieving its head.

"I know this is asking a lot." She blushed, a cross between shy and embarrassed, as she aligned herself neck to…neck. "Could you help me with the ribbon?"

Ardruina, this unearthly being, that beheaded tech bros like it was nothing…

Needed him.

Shoving the part of him that wanted to scream and run away into a box, Theodore threw away the key. Then, he found the green ribbon near where her head had been, and after brushing pine needles from her cheek with a trembling hand, he wrapped the ribbon around her neck and tied it in a neat, tight bow.

God, how's that gonna stay on?

He wrung his hands, certain they were both in denial.

When she let go, he shot forward, palms outstretched, ready to catch her head, but she just stretched and cracked her neck, full motion returned.

Thank Jesus. He never wanted to see her head fall off ever again.

"Better?" He meant to sound composed and suave. Instead, the question came out in a mousey squeak.

"Much." She nodded, casting a look about, taking in the carnage.

They'd have to clean this up.

Bending down, Theodore lifted one of the decapitated heads. "Oh gosh, I forgot how heavy these things were," he gagged, almost dropping it. Everything was weird and clammy and if he looked at it, he'd hurl, so he didn't.

Ardruina smirked, joining him in body disposal. "You do this often?"

"Well, no," he replied, chucking goon #1's head into the bog. *Splat.* Sucking mud pulled it down with a loud, ugly belch. "I meant the trivia."

"That seems truer to character."

"You look like you've chopped off heads before."

"Only those who deserved it." And then after a moment, "I'm not going to chop your head off, Theodore."

Cool.

"So, um, I don't mean to sound rude or ungrateful—you did rescue me twice in two days, which wow, I'm shaping up to be a real damsel in distress, aren't I?"

"Theodore," she said softly, cutting off his rambling. "You can just ask. It won't offend me."

"What… who are you?"

"Have you ever heard of The Wild Huntsman? Or the Dullahan?"

"That's Irish folklore, right?"

She nodded. "Mhmm. But the first one's German."

"Oh, I forgot about that. Like in the Legend of Sleepy Hollow."

"Just like that." Her answering smile was playfully impish. "I was heading north, on my way here, at the time."

Oh. *Ohhh.*

A bona fide, supernatural legend. He already knew Ardruina was way out of his league. This defied comprehension.

And then she blew him a kiss, and his hopeless heart melted into a puddle of goop.

Piece after piece, they fed the bog their feast of misdeeds, knowing Dead Man's Hollow would hold onto their secrets and never let go.

Sabotage gone wrong. Murder. Almost dying, *again*. A centuries-old, sometimes-headless lover. There was so much to process, but one thing stood out, one feeling that outshone them all.

"I can't tell you how glad I am you're not dead."

When Theodore took Ardruina's hand, she smiled.

EPILOGUE

ONE YEAR LATER

Something in the bog watched. A centuries-old being lurked in its depths, claiming heads wherever she found them. With one brutal stroke of the arm, she cut down even the strongest…

"Teddy?"

Theodore sighed, rising from the ground on stiff knees. "Sweetheart, I know you can be scary. I've seen it."

"I would, but it's just this contraption." Ardruina giggled. "Lady Crane is scandalized."

"Lady Crane has no idea." He folded his arms across his bare chest, keeping his back turned. Couldn't spoil the surprise.

"All right. All right. Let's try again."

Hoofbeats retreated, until the only sounds left were the ones the bog provided. Rustling wind, the gurgling, squelching flow of water.

Theodore crouched down, studying the sundews before him. One of its mauls closed around some unlucky insect. *To have and to hold. To hold and to feed.* And the bog kept their secrets well.

The draining project stopped when Leon Marks disappeared. No money, no construction, no resort. There was an investigation, of course. Local law enforcement combed through the town, the bog, looking for the missing billionaire. They never turned up anything. It helped that an insider trading allegation against Marks came out within days of his demise, along with other white-collar crimes, and people just assumed he got a tipoff, fled the United States, and disappeared on the dime of an offshore bank account and foreign oligarch friends.

That suited Theodore and Ardruina just fine. Dead Man's Hollow was protected land now.

The quiet was interrupted by rapidly approaching hoofbeats. Nothing living should have such purchase on unsolid terrain, and yet it was quickly gaining ground.

Theodore chanced a glance over his shoulder, only to find a shadowy figure barreling down upon him on a white, mud-speckled horse.

He shot up from the ground and ran, all thirty-plus years of bog geography firmly mapped out in his mind. It wasn't the most direct route back to his cottage, but it was the safest. Even where the ground was its firmest and driest, mud still squished beneath his shoes. When he slipped, he counterbalanced. When he fell, he ignored the cold water that seeped into his joggers, the shriek of the horse, and its bloodthirsty rider. He just scrambled to his feet, and kept going, never once looking back.

Theodore pumped his arms and legs, bringing his knees up high just as his one-time coach had shouted. He wasn't strong but he was fast, and nimble, once a midfielder for his collegiate club soccer team.

But outrun a horse?

Nothing had ever trained him for that.

He ran through the pain, heart racing, lungs burning. Not for anything would he stop. His very life depended on it. The thunderous charge behind him was the nightmare he kept pace to, the horse's harsh, panting breaths hot against his back.

Too close, much too close.

Theodore sped for the bog's edge, for the safety of his cabin. He'd been a friend to Dead Man's Hollow all his life, had fought for its very survival. Tonight was not the night he met his demise at the hands of the formidable being that stalked its shadows.

Fifty feet. Forty. Thirty.

The sodden, open landscape firmed beneath his feet, a strip of forest land just ahead, the bog's edge closing in. He saw his cottage between the trees and the screen door that promised sanctuary, if only he reached it in time.

Twenty feet.

A streak of white rushed past him, lifting the hairs on the back of his neck and arms. He didn't stop. It wasn't over until it was over.

Blood pumped in his ears and lactic acid burned his thighs as his lungs screamed for oxygen.

Ten feet.

The horse reared beside him, and let out a bloodcurdling, battle-field screech, its rider a shadow haunting his periphery.

Theodore slammed bodily into the door, only breaking momentum now, because with an adversary hot on his heels, every single second before had mattered. Wrenching the door open, he squirreled himself inside, and latched it shut.

He backed away from the door, hands on his thighs, sucking in deep lungsful of air. *No longer in the bog. Nothing can touch you here. Not in your own home.*

What happens in the bog stays in the bog. Those were the rules.

And he made it, he made it home.

Past the pounding of his own racing heart, it was quiet outside, his backyard suspiciously empty, as if his purser had never existed. Only the sound of birds and crickets performing their evening symphony broke that eerie stillness.

He won. He outran the Headless Horsewoman of Dead Man's Hollow.

Winning never felt more like losing.

A tall figure darkened his threshold, and before he could so much as blink, she kicked open his door, splintered wood flying.

Theodore jolted back with a surprised squeak, fumbling for some-thing, anything, to create a barrier.

The door banged against the wall, hanging cockeyed on its hinges from the sheer force behind the kick, and all he grabbed was a broom handle. Warmth bloomed in his cheeks…

And lower.

He was royally fucked.

Before he could so much as protest, Ardruina smacked the broom from his hands and grabbed him by his waistband, hauling him into the bedroom. She pushed him toward the bed. The back of his knees hit the edge, and he sat down with a heavy *oof*.

"Submit to me, human, and I will spare you."

Theodore met her dark brown eyes, glittering with mirth, a contrast to the rest of her appearance, all power and danger. She wore black riding leathers, tattered and weather-worn, and her curls haloed her head in a dark wind-swept cloud. Just like the day they met.

Well. Almost.

There was one pants-immolating difference.

The harness gracing her hips, and the purple phallus jutting from between her thighs.

Well fuck me.

She smirked. Words hadn't passed between them, but she knew. And she would. "Take those filthy pants off."

Kicking off his shoes, Theodore was all too eager to comply. His joggers hit the floor next.

A fierce glint flashed across her eyes, and the smirk grew as she twirled her finger. "Hands and knees, Theodore."

Oh boy, he was in trouble. He turned and crawled to the center of the bed. The best kind of trouble.

It wasn't his first time bottoming, nor would it be his last, but it was his first time with her.

She smoothed her gloved hands over his ass, leather on bare skin, before yanking him back by the hips to the edge. Theodore fell forward, chest hitting the mattress, leaving his ass high in the air and hard-on dangling between his legs. Dammit if he wasn't going to stay here on display with his face comfortably pillowed.

A feast for the taking.

Ardruina knelt behind him, hands still at his hips, and trailed her nose along the back of his thigh. "Lavender." She inhaled deeply.

It was a wonder she could still smell the soap he used after his sprint through the bog, but Theodore wasn't about to look a gift horse in the mouth. He spent a good part of his morning routine on hair removal, too. "Your favorite."

"My favorite," she agreed, purring against his skin.

Teeth grazed, then nipped at the firm flesh of his backside. Her strong fingers dug in, holding Theodore right where she wanted him, and he was completely at her mercy as she delved her tongue between his thighs. A swipe here, a swipe there, from perineum to stern, until her wet, probing tongue reached that tight little hole, circling it round and round.

A shiver ran through him, almost tickling from her soft, wet attentions. He didn't have to pretend with Ardruina. Didn't have to be bigger, stronger, or anything other than what he was and that went both ways. She embraced all of him, and he embraced all of her, head-tumbling and all.

Ardruina stroked down with her fingers, teasing the underside of his shaft, the light touch filling his limbs with sweet anticipation. He twitched, eager and ready.

Then she withdrew her hand, leaving his aching dick unattended.

He groaned in protest.

"Theodore," she growled. "Where are your manners?"

"Manners?" His voice was muffled by the comforter. He didn't expend the effort to raise his head.

"If you want something, ask for it nicely." She snaked a hand around, gently tugging his balls, and *fuck*, he would've liked that hand wrapped around his dick instead.

And she would, if he asked, but that wasn't the point of this game. "I want to be at your mercy."

Her dark chuckle eclipsed any doubt; she knew the rules perfectly well. "Oh you most certainly are."

She spread his ass wide, gliding her tongue up, then pushing in. It wasn't a deep penetration, but it consumed all thought, everything revolving around that one exquisite point of contact. She rubbed the outer ring with her thumb, teasing the edge made slick by her tongue, before reaching to the nightstand beside them.

Behind him, a plastic bottle lid snapped open, a drizzle of cool liquid following down the cleft of his ass. Ardruina coated her thumb in it, gently probing past the tight ring of muscle and slipping the digit inside. Theodore melted into the soft bed, arching and spreading himself so Arduina could reach deeper.

A breathy moan escaped his lips when she finally, *finally*, wrapped a hand around his aching hard-on. Theodore lost himself to sensation as Ardruina worked him from both ends, drawing him to the brink of release.

But he never got to tip over that edge.

Ardruina withdrew all contact and stood abruptly, leaving him empty and gasping.

He heard the squeeze of the bottle again, so he snuck a look behind him, finding Ardruina stroking lube over the purple phallus, her leather-clad hand working it back and forth. *Fuck*, that was mesmerizing.

She met his eye. "Keep watching."

He was about to get railed by his girl. He couldn't look away if he tried.

She stepped between his legs, rubbing the phallus up and down his ass. "You're mine."

"I'm yours." Since the day she revealed her secret to save his life. Who she was, *what* she was—a Dullahan, a headless horsewoman— they wouldn't be here if it weren't for that.

Ardruina's detachable head? And their staggering, centuries-long age gap? It took some getting used to, that's for certain, but Theodore loved her strength and power. Her *otherworldliness*. None of those things should be hidden. Not for him. Not for anyone.

She gripped his hips, watching his face closely as she pressed in. Behind the wicked mirth glittering in those coal-black eyes lay a hint of caution. He knew what she looked for—pleasure, discomfort—all the things he paid attention to when their roles were reversed.

"Keep going," he whispered, not wanting her to balk at the initial resistance. "That's it."

He repeated the encouragement, each iteration sounding more and more like a moan, until she was seated to the hilt. "You feel so good, sweetheart."

She issued a shallow test thrust.

He bit his lower lip. "Mmph. More."

She thrust again, deeper this time, and her eyelids fluttered closed —a jolt of pleasure taking them both. The toy they chose was designed to deliver clitoral stimulation with each thrust, so she could enjoy this as much as he did. "I like where this hits."

"Me too."

She banded an arm around his chest and with rough jerk, hauled him into an upright position, bringing him flush with her body. She smoothed the palm of her hand down his torso, to where he ached for more. He gripped her thighs, fingers digging into her leather riding gear, as her hips and hand worked him in tandem.

If she kept this up, it wouldn't be long before he came.

He was already wound tight, almost ready to blow.

"I want to try something, Teddy." His heart lurched at the endearment. It wasn't often that she called him "Teddy." Only when his terrifying beauty felt vulnerable. But she didn't need to be afraid. Not with him. Not when the thought of trying new things with her excited him beyond measure.

"Okay." His pulse quickened, half alive with anticipation, half afraid he'd come too soon. Depending on what this "something new" was, it could all be over in the next ten seconds. "What is it, sweetheart?"

She stilled—her hips, the stroking of his dick—and...*dammit.* Why'd she have to stop? That brink she brought him so excruciatingly close to for the second time ebbed away. If he weren't dying to know what she had in mind, he might've growled in frustration. And when she completely removed her hands from his body, he couldn't imagine what in the sweet hell she had planned for him.

Whatever it was, he didn't think he could survive another round of edging.

Unless…

Something rustled behind him. "Hold out your hand."

A thrill shot up his spine at the possibilities, Ardruina's torturous designs quickly forgiven. Was it another toy? A cock ring, perhaps?

It was nothing he expected. It was more. So much more.

Green silk ribbon whispered against his palm. Theodore curled his fingers protectively around it, his heart beating thunderously against his ribcage. What Ardruina placed in his care was worth far more than anything that could be bought.

This ribbon fused Ardruina's head to her body with a magic Theodore couldn't even begin to comprehend. All he needed to know was that if it was ever stolen, lost, or destroyed, her head would be detached forever. It wouldn't kill her, but it would make her vulnerable. If someone took her head, they could use it to control her. Make her do their bidding.

Only a gift of this magnitude could be earned. That Ardruina would trust him with something so precious…

"Sweetheart," he breathed, his heart swelling with emotion.

This was why she stopped, why she let go. She needed her hands to hold her head.

"Wrap it around your neck," she whispered, her voice carrying lower than it did before, and off to the side. He couldn't be sure without looking, but if he had to guess, she was cradling her head under an arm. "Just once. Leave the ends untied in the back."

With trembling fingers, he followed her instructions, wrapping the ribbon around his neck like a choker, but leaving the ends to trail down his back.

Oh, how he needed this. *Needed her.*

"Teddy," she purred, curling her fingers around the ends of the green ribbon like reins and pulling tight. Her voice moved—behind him, beside him, then beneath him. "Hold me."

He carefully took her head into his hands, palms cupping her cheeks. She grinned up at him, a cheeky, sultry twist to her purple lips.

"Good boys get kisses."

His breath hitched. "You sure?"

The ribbon tightened around his neck. "Don't make me tell you again."

It didn't matter that he held Ardruina's head in his hands, the power to command and control. He was at her mercy.

Theodore cradled her head between his thighs, nearly combusting when she took him into her mouth. With her fingers wound tight around the ribbon, her other hand at his hip, she began to thrust again, pushing him deep into her mouth.

He rocked between those dual points of blinding pleasure, shifting his gaze between the ceiling and the wicked glint in her eyes. Oh god, oh god, he was not going to last. He had one, two, maybe three…

Ardruina shuddered behind him, her eyelids fluttering closed.

Fuuuck.

He squeezed his eyes shut as he came, lips parting on a tattered exhale. His whole body thrummed with release, and he emptied into her hot, eager mouth, relishing the feel of her tongue curled around him.

Several beats passed between them as they both panted in tandem. Then, Ardruina released her hold on the ribbon and took back her head.

Theodore fell forward on his hands and knees, over the wet spot on the bedding where his cum had leaked. He slapped a hand to his neck, catching the green ribbon before it slipped.

The bed creaked as Ardruina withdrew and stepped off the edge.

It had only been a handful of seconds, but Theodore found himself turning, searching for her eyes, needing to see how she felt in the aftermath. Dark brown eyes met his blue as she affixed her head to her neck, all wickedness gone, replaced by tenderness.

Words didn't pass between them. Theodore just walked on his knees to the edge of the bed, threading the green ribbon around her neck, his fingers grazing her skin as he went. It felt like a raised scar, the place where her head and neck met.

"I really like you, Theodore." She murmured softly, holding still as he retied the green ribbon. "And I want to keep you for as long as I can."

"I'm right here. Not going anywhere."

"No, I know. It's…" She smoothed her hands down his chest, then wrapped her arms around his waist, holding him close. "I know a werebear that comes this way each spring. If you wanted longevity, I could catch her on her next trip down and ask her to…" She trailed off, gaze dropping. A pink flush tinged her ghostly pale cheeks.

He grinned so wide his cheeks hurt. "Sweetheart, are you asking me to become your *Teddy Bear?*"

She rolled her eyes and lightly punched his shoulder. A broad, uncharacteristically shy smile overtook her face. "Maybe."

"I think you more than like me." He tipped her chin up, placing a soft, sweet kiss to her lips. "If you're looking for ways to extend my lifespan."

She hugged him like she never wanted to let go. "Well, I love you, Teddy."

"I love you, too." No hesitation. It wasn't even a question.

"Even with what I am, and what I've done?"

Protecting this bog. Protecting him.

Undeniably.

"Especially." He tucked a wayward curl behind her ear. "I've always loved pretty, vicious things."

AUTHOR'S NOTE

Now that you've finished reading, I can finally say which two classic horror stories I mashed together to create *The Feast of Dead Man's Hollow*. This story combines "The Legend of Sleepy Hollow" with "The Girl with the Green Ribbon"—both spoilers if you're a horror genre reader—but it gender-bends the former while also giving Jenny, the female character in the latter, the agency and badassery she deserves through Ardruina.

That we all deserve.

The Feast of Dead Man's Hollow originally appeared as a short story in the *Crimson Bones* anthology by Brigids Gate Press. The rights have since reverted to me, giving me the opportunity to expand Teddy and Ardruina's romance. Apart from the epilogue, all the main events are the same, but we dive deeper into the characters' emotions.

I tried expanding the story beyond its original scope several times, and let's be honest, it could've been a whole book. There was an opportunity to draw out the conflict with Leon Marks, but each time I tried I felt the couple's unique charm slipping away. And really, do we want to put up with billionaires any more than we already do?

That's why *The Feast of Dead Man's Hollow* is more of a novelette. Or a spooky smut pamphlet. When Teddy and Ardruina said, "Hey!

This is our story," I had to listen. If you're a writer, you know how it is. The characters get the final say.

On the heels of my Harlequin monster romance release *Untethering Dark*, I've been anxious about following it up, worried I just can't top Astrid and Gudarīks. It's like the sophomore novel scaries, only this will be my seventh book. Turns out, new release nerves never go away.

But it's not about topping the last book. Just writing something fun and enjoying the process. If Teddy gets to enjoy some pegging along the way, well then, I guess there *was* some "topping" after all ;)

ACKNOWLEDGMENTS

Agatha Andrews, the host of the She Wore Black Podcast, was the first to read *The Feast of Dead Man's Hollow* in its original short story format. Her love for the story gave me the confidence to submit it, then expand and re-release it.

My beta readers and brainstorming buddies continue to be amazing. I wouldn't be able to do what I do without them. Thank you—Alexandra, Ally, Chanel, Dani, Katie Erin, Kyle, Laura, Morgan, and Seffra—for your time and incredible insight. And thank you Jess Armstrong for the final, eleventh-hour horror/romance vibe check.

ABOUT THE AUTHOR

By night, Desirée M. Niccoli writes a blend of vicious romance and cozy horror, featuring monsters, villains, and the supernatural, often served with (mostly) emotionally intelligent characters and heart. By day, she is a public relations professional living the nomadic military life with her husband and two cats Pawdry Hepburn and Puma Thurman. Although born and raised in Pittsburgh, Desirée has since lived in coastal Maine (where her spooky heart truly lies), Maryland, and Connecticut.

Want to be the first to get a look at covers, sneak peeks, and more? Sign up for her newsletter and find out more at www.dmniccoli.com.

PUBLISHED WORKS

Untethering Dark
Follow Me to the Yew Tree
Given to the Ghoul

Haven Cove series
Called to the Deep
Song of Lorelei
Ensnaring the Siren

BUT WAIT, THERE'S MORE

If you like supernatural ladies with secrets,
read on for the beginning of
Follow Me to the Yew Tree.

PREVIEW: FOLLOW ME TO THE YEW TREE

CHAPTER 1

I'm a long way from home.

I've exchanged Éire's rugged coast for a far-swept moor, and I don't know why I've been sent, only that I'm needed. And I'm nothing if not a faithful servant.

The road's been quiet—I haven't seen another soul in days—but now there's a lone man on horseback heading West, toward me.

All he has is what can be carried on his horse—bedroll, canvas tent, a saddle bag presumably filled with provisions. A cutlass dangles from one hip, a pistol is strapped to the other, and I've met enough sailors to know they are Navy-issue.

Auburn curls frosted white roll across his brow, ruffled by the breeze, the first splotch of color upon a drab landscape. With proper sunlight, the moor's green and purple grasses might've been better served, but today it's overcast and drizzling.

He tips his head in polite greeting, the small gold hoop in his ear catching the muted light. To say it glinted would be generous. Compared to the tattered, blue frock coat he wears with scuffed navy buttons and cuffs frayed and salt stained, or the tarnished compass that hangs from his belt, it's the most polished thing about him.

He doesn't smile as our eyes meet, and yet a gentle wave of warmth settles in my chest, dripping slow and syrupy as honey. It's a bizarre sensation. Usually, when I find the one I'm meant to meet, the emotions strike cold and harsh. Why this is different, I can't say, and it doesn't begin to make any more sense even as a glowing vision follows.

It hits so suddenly my eyes swim with tears, as if I've dared to stare at the sun. Squinting and blinking doesn't help, but eventually my sight clears on its own, giving way to two distinctly recognizable figures.

They stand beneath the twisted boughs of a tree, their hands clasped, and heads bowed, backlit by an early morning sun. Beneath their bare feet, the moor grasses are still damp and glittering with dew.

Years of knowing imbue that touch, one of people whose understanding is marrow deep. And maybe that explains why their clothing is unfamiliar. Why it displays a scandalous amount of skin neither acknowledge. It's a glimpse at the times to come, a time when fabric molds and accentuates the body rather than hides it.

His lips curl into a sweet smile as he gazes at her mouth. Whatever he whispers brings a bright flush to her pale white cheeks, but she rises on her toes, boldly closing the distance. Her raven-dark hair is ever shifting, blown about on some ghostly breeze, and her eyes are a paler green than the Lily of the Valley that grows in the tree's shade.

He captures her face in both hands, the words "Hold Fast" inked across his fingers, sailors tattoos, as much a part of him as the calluses on his palm that now scrape across her cheeks. *It's not the first time they've done this, but he slowly sips at her mouth, savoring her like it is, stroking the column of her throat with his thumbs. It's a tender dance of lips pursued by the languid glide of tongue, and the easy tempo endures even when he presses her against the tree, trapping her body with his own. The way he sucks her lower lip into his mouth, tugging lightly with his teeth, is so deliciously obscene, it's a surprise when he abruptly pulls away, leaving her red and swollen.*

His eyes hold hers as he sucks two of his fingers into his mouth, cheeks hollowing out, before pulling the wet digits free and reaching down. It takes so very little effort to get beneath the skirt she wears. A garment that falls above the knee, not below.

Everything is quiet save for birdsong and soft, hitched gasps.

The vision's gone in a flash, a snapshot in time that leaves me breathless and stunned. It takes me a moment too long to realize I've been given a glimpse of the future. Of *my* future.

I see much but never something intimate. And never for me.

My horse whickers nervously, yanking me back into the present. I pat its neck, murmuring soothing words, even as my cheeks burn. "There, there. All is well."

I've never had reason to doubt my visions before, but if this one's to be trusted, the frowning man on the road ahead is my paramour-to-be.

Is this why I was sent? A reward for my centuries of faithful service? A balm to ease the weight of endless days and the long road ahead?

Hope burns bright in my chest. After witnessing so much pain and suffering, here's finally something good to hold onto. Someone to cherish, to keep. To call my own.

Love is the greatest gift of all, and if it's been gifted to me, I am well-appreciated indeed. All these long centuries spent grieving may finally be worth something, culminating to this moment.

Our horses draw near. I'm close enough to the man that I spy the constellation of freckles spanning his nose and the slight widening of dark brown eyes. Perhaps I stare too long because he hastily looks away, eyes bashfully averted, weather-and age-worn cheeks blooming a rosy color.

He couldn't have seen the vision. Could he?

Glancing down at myself, I'm quickly reminded of the fact that my long skirts are pulled up in front, revealing the men's riding trousers worn underneath. No skin is exposed, but well-regarded ladies don't dress as such.

There's nothing for it. Comfort and practicality must supersede some conventions.

I clear my throat and say, "Tráthnóna maith."

He looks up, surprised. Perhaps it's been a long time since he's heard the language of home. Seems just like the sort of thing a British naval officer would forbid, and I mourn the loss. "Tráthnóna maith." The surprise quickly dissipates, replaced by a flash of grim, troubled panic before falling into a more neutral expression. Did he not want to be recognized? "You're a long way from home."

"So are you."

A pause. His horse snorts, impatiently side-stepping.

"How did you know?" he asks.

"I had a feeling." What I don't say is that I wouldn't be here in this foreign country, sent to find him, if we didn't share a homeland. Éire, the place the English call *Ireland*.

A dark pallor drops over his face, obscuring his features in shadow. It's not an expression, or a change in mood, but a sign. A sign only I can see, and the warm feeling in my chest chills. He's not the first I've seen bearing such a portend, not by far, and he won't be the last. But after that beautiful, promising vision, I thought he was meant to be mine.

I thought I had a future that wasn't steeped only in sorrow.

I never should've assumed this meeting would end any differently than what's come before, that the one I serve would deign to bestow a gift. One pretty vision doesn't mean I know the man, or have any right to him, but to dangle hope and possibility in front of me like this, only to yank it away is unusually cruel.

It's all I can do to keep my voice even when I ask, "What's your name, sailor?"

His jaw clenches, and a haunted look steals the light from his eyes. "Don't."

I stiffen, taking him in. His eyes all at once turn wary and weary. He's a bit paler, too, beneath the damning shadow that hovers over his face.

"I'm not...I didn't choose that," he says.

I know that look. I've seen it before.

Many young men were impressed into His Majesty's Royal Navy during the Napoleonic Wars. Some are returning, but many will not.

Just knowing this is the pain his past holds, calls to the part of me that wants to offer comfort, but never can. That doesn't mean I won't try. "I'm sorry. How long?"

"Too long. Enough to appoint me Gunner on a Man O' War."

"I take it that's not an easy accomplishment."

"From landsmen? Shouldn't've been possible, but enough men die on a ship, and someone's got to step in, take a place they never would've filled before. Many years of learning the hard way and eventually someone notices and decides it's worth something."

"Was it worth something to you?" I ask softly. In this, his opinion is the only one that matters.

He gives the question some thought, brows pinched, before answering, "Better pension, maybe." He frowns. "But I don't consider the proficiency of my position an accomplishment."

More death.

We're quiet for a long while, wind whipping about the moor grasses. I watch them sway. They remind me of waves, and I wonder if that thought crosses his mind, too.

"Elin," he says after a time. "That's my name. Da was an Englishman with a sense of humor." He runs a hand through his curls, burnished red against roughened, inked knuckles. "Like the sound, though."

A grown man with a name usually given to girls. While it's Welsh for "shining light," I can't decide if his father's humor is cruel or something else, but I like the sound, too, despite it.

Nodding to his horse, I say, "You're taking the long way home."

"If I never see another ship again, it will be too soon." There's a hint of wry humor to his words, a reluctant acknowledgement that he will eventually have to sail again if he's to make it the rest of the way home, hopping from one island to the next.

"It must be a relief to be on solid ground again." It's not a particularly insightful response, but it's the first one to come to mind, and I find myself wanting to hear more of his voice and its gruff timbre.

Tipping his head back, and baring his face to the sky, Elin breathes in deep, serenity falling over his features. It's an open expression that softens the lines of his face, shaving away years of hardship, making him almost beautiful. When he finds my eyes once more, his are glittering coals closer to onyx than brown. "It's all I've wanted, even if it's not my own."

We're quiet a moment before Elin asks, "How is it at home, now that the war's done?" His voice is hesitant, as if he's afraid to know the answer.

I wish I could assuage his fears, but he's right to be worried.

Our country is in recession.

Manufacturing has decreased. Merchants are falling bankrupt, leaving so many unemployed, and what employment there still is comes at the cost of steeply slashed wages.

During the war, Éire supplied the English with beef, pork, and grain, but now that Napoleon has been defeated, competition from foreign exporters has made our trade dismal. Éire is no longer England's sole granary, and with the demand down, our farmers are already suffering. And so, so many of our people are farmers.

His expression darkens. My lack of a ready answer is telling. "It's not good, is it?"

"No, it's not." And even harder times ahead. It's a pattern with which I'm woefully familiar; centuries of living have taught me that war, famine, plague, and death are frequently grim companions.

Crop failure is coming. The next two years will yield so little, the people will dig out and eat their seed potatoes in desperation and be forced to scrounge for nettles and wild vegetables, whatever they can do to put something in their aching bellies. But it won't be enough.

It's a future filled with so many ghostly faces, people with sunken cheeks, and hollow, haunted eyes. If starvation doesn't claim them, fever and disease will.

"It's difficult to find work," I add, reluctantly. As a frequent bearer of bad news, you'd think I'd be used to it, but I loathe sharing this information. His homecoming should be a cause for celebration, joy. "Manufacturing and farming's not looking good."

He sighs. "Not sure they'll be keen, but I suppose the lads coming home can be fishermen."

I wince, and he notices, jaw clenching. "That, too?" he asks.

"Afraid so."

His expression is grim, resigned. "Seems the war has found a way to keep killing us after all."

I wish I could offer him comforting words, some sort of reassurance, but I've none to give. There's nothing left to do but march forward and make the very best of it as we can. I gesture behind me from the way I came. "I was just about to turn around. Mind if I join you?"

Elin tenses, his horse pawing at the ground. "Suppose you must, if we're headed the same way."

So much for clasped hands and heated kisses. I've no right to feel hurt by his lack of enthusiasm, but it stings, nonetheless. With a light jerk on the reins in my hands, I spin my mount around to lead the way. "I'm not such bad company." Might not be what he's expecting, a lone woman on an unmarked road, but I'm not unpleasant, and we share a language and a homeland.

He follows. "I meant no offense. It's just, I've traveled a long time alone."

If his crew didn't count—those that survived, that is—it must've been a long time indeed. My feelings aren't made of stone, but I take his meaning.

We ride in silence, miles passing through mountain and glen, the light of an already dim sky falling toward night. It's a peaceful kind of quiet, the kind that should only come from knowing someone a long time, or perhaps the things Elin has seen have made his spirit as old as mine.

As the sun dips near the horizon, my new travel companion brings his horse to a stop.

"Let's make camp." He angles toward a copse of trees, as if called by instinct to buttress against something firm, rather than boldly claiming open ground.

The shadowy pallor still hangs over his face, a grim warning of doom to come, but it hasn't worsened. Whatever's coming isn't imminent. Not yet anyway.

Casting a surveying look around just to be sure, I sense nothing amiss and follow without a word. Here is as good as any.

Elin takes the lead, tending to the horses and setting up a simple, canvas tent. He tackles each task swiftly and efficiently, the years at sea having done nothing to dull his landside skills.

He's busy unfurling a bedroll when he says, "I can take one side, you the other."

A generous offer to a stranger. Or maybe it's because I'm a woman and some chivalrous need dictates the gesture. As I unstrap the bedroll from my saddle, I feel the weight of his eyes on me, their presence warming me from behind. I'm not sure why I like that he looks, or why I like it even more that he doesn't avert his gaze when I turn around, his assessment continuing from a comfortable distance away.

"What brings you out here?" He watches me carefully, cautiously, like he might not wholly trust my intentions.

My inner turmoil returns. He's right to be wary. Why had I been sent? And what good were visions of a future that would never come true?

"I haven't figured that out yet." It's evasive, but also the truth as I know it, and I want to put him at ease, even if I'm beset by uncertainty. "But it's nice to have company for once."

A tiny smile lifts the corners of his lips, so it must work. "You wander often?"

"Spent a lot of time along Éire's east coast—Wicklow, Dublin—wherever I'm needed. I'm part of a courier service of sorts."

His brow ticks up a fraction. "Would I know it?" There's something teasing now about his tone.

I shrug.

"Do you like what you do?"

"Depends on the day. These are hard times. But on the good ones, I like to think I'm preparing people, letting them know what's to come. No one likes to be completely caught off guard."

Elin's smile fades. "No, I don't think we do."

While I arrange my bedroll inside the tent, contemplating overlong on the narrow space between mine and his, he gathers wood and builds a fire. By the time he's done a sheen of sweat coats his forehead, his cheeks pale. Before I can ask if he's feeling okay, he curtly excuses himself, snatching a saddle bag from the ground as he stalks tightly away into the dark of night.

Some call of nature beckons him away, but it isn't any of my business.

When he returns, he seems less strained, but his color hasn't returned, and his movements seem heavier. I dig into my rations. The bread I hand him in small chunks shouldn't be as fresh as it is, but he doesn't question it. Just murmurs his thanks and takes the first piece, popping it into his mouth, eyes closing, before chewing and swallowing. Bits of smoked, dried meat follow.

He eats a little but declines the rest. "I'm turning in."

There's no reason to sit here alone, not when curiosity about this man pulls at my chest.

He doesn't even turn around, just holds open the tent flap to let me in after him.

We shuck our shoes and lay down, tucking into our separate spaces—him on the left, me the right. Under the cover of my blanket, I slip out of the men's trousers, and though I try to be discreet about it, Elin's skyward stare is much too deliberate, his cheeks pink. Something about his shyness plucks at my heartstrings. There's so little between us in this shared space, and for all that society would consider me a woman of ill-repute just for the pragmatic way I dress, this land-starved sailor is respecting my privacy.

Even though it's not me who's shy, I leave the rest of my clothing be, and settle in.

Elin's lashes flutter, then fall closed, and he does a little shimmy getting into a more comfortable position.

We are close. So close I can feel his heat. I'd only need to turn over my arm to touch him, but I don't.

His breathing softens, deepens. Just when I think he's fallen asleep, he asks, "What's your name?"

"I've had many."

"Your favorite?"

I think a moment. "Éireann."

"Will I see you in the morning?"

An odd question. Where was there to go in the middle of the night? Did he think I was a thief? That I would steal his things and run off while he slept? Surely, he wouldn't have invited me to sleep next to him if he suspected that. "You'll see me in the morning."

Burrowing beneath his blanket, he turns over, back facing me. I know there's trust in that, but it makes my heart twinge, nonetheless. "In that case, oíche mhaith, Éireann."

"Oíche mhaith."

PREVIEW CONTINUED: FOLLOW ME TO THE YEW TREE

CHAPTER 2

A pressure on my bladder rouses me, but I pull up my blanket to cover my nose against the early morning chill. I'm reluctant to crack open my eyes, because the moment I do the pleasant dream I had will be gone.

"Be very still." Elin's voice is calm and quiet but firm.

My eyes fly open.

He's crouched beside me, a finger pressed to his lips. The shadowy pallor over his face is still there, but it hasn't worsened overnight, which eases some of my worry. "We've got company," he murmurs. "But I've got you. Just be very still."

And then I feel it. A wriggling between my left leg and the crease made by the tent's canvas and the ground. Without so much as twitching a muscle, my gaze dips down. There's an adder tucked half in, half out of my sleeping roll. Hardy and long-living, I may be, but not invincible, and I'm one venomous bite away from a bad day.

"What should I do?"

Picking up his blanket, and holding it between his hands, Elin answers, "Just slowly slide toward me. Don't jostle or squish it."

I do as he says, slowly inching my body across the ground until I'm pressed against his legs in the cramped space. For all that I'm one false move away from being bitten, a small thrill tingles in my belly at the contact. The vision of his lips on mine, thumbs stroking my neck, infiltrates my thoughts, insistent I don't forget. And how could I? It haunted my dreams in the dead of night, the sweetest, most persistent torture.

"Okay, slowly sit up," he instructs, his eyes never leaving the snake.

When I've done it, he continues, "Now get up and back out of the tent."

I like the command of his voice, and the assurance that it gives. It keeps me calm. As long as he's here, I'm safe, and I desperately want to offer him the same in return.

The snake is indifferent to my exit, just slides the rest of its body into the warm spot I vacated. Elin gingerly backs out. Together, we stare at the tent awhile, saying nothing, the air brisk.

"Wanted my body heat." I shiver, rubbing my arms.

"Mm." He nods, draping his blanket around my shoulders. "Were you bit? Anything hurt?"

I shake my head.

"We should check, just in case."

Putting ample distance between myself and the tent, I sit down on the ground, and he follows, crossing his legs. As I pull up my skirt, just enough to expose my calf and lower thigh, pale white flesh on display, my heart skips a beat. If the future's to be trusted, he will one day see all this and more.

If he's tempted by what he sees, he doesn't show it.

Brow furrowed in studious concentration, Elin rubs his hands together, then cups them over his mouth, blowing hot air. He repeats this process a few more times. When he places his hands on me, one behind my knee, the other my calf, they're warm and assured. Although he'd averted his eyes to my partial undressing the night before, he's not shy now as he examines and rotates my leg, pausing once to brush a finger over two beauty marks north of my knee.

Determining them innocuous, he moves on, palms skimming bare flesh.

The skin-to-skin contact is more comforting than I could've ever imagined, and there's a pleasant, buzzing sensation racing up my limbs and settling in my chest. It's no wonder humans seek touch so arduously; Elin hasn't yet let go, and I'm already craving more.

"No bite marks," he concludes, knees cracking as he rises to his feet.

I lower my dress and hold out my hand. Even though I don't need the help, I'm a newly made glutton. His grasp is firm as he pulls me to my feet.

Clutching the ends of the blanket to my chest, I nod toward the tent. "Now what?"

"Snake stays as long as it wants," is all he says, before setting off to gather kindling.

We leave when the snake does. It's a later start than either of us intended, but we manage six miles by midday. Elin is a quiet companion, but I like his presence.

When he takes a drink from his canteen, and wordlessly passes it to me, I notice the shadowy pall over him has darkened.

Alarm stabs in my chest, my eyes swimming with unbidden tears. In my haste to dry them , I'm clumsy with the canteen and spill our water. There's a wail, too, building in my diaphragm that I forcibly suppress. A bad, bad sign.

"You okay?"

"Gnat in my eye," I lie, trying to discreetly scan our surroundings for a threat.

He offers a handkerchief, and I take it, making a show of wiping an eye.

The vision that follows is fuzzy at the edges—a clear sign what I see isn't set in stone, at least not yet. It's a warning, and one I know I should convey, to give him time to prepare. It's why I'm here, after all, why I must've been assigned to him, but this can't be the end, not when we've barely begun. And not after all he's endured. To survive a war only to die on the journey home, that's not fate, it's cruelty. There should be so much life ahead of him to live. He deserves so much more than what this one is giving him.

But what if…

What if there's a silver lining to these visions? What if knowing what will happen ahead of time means I can stop it? What if I can save Elin?

It's not a thought I've had before. But I have to try.

There's two ways what comes next could play out, three if I'm quick enough.

But before the vision fully clears from my eyes, and before I can warn him, Elin is shouting. His horse rears, spooked by the snake I now know to be slithering through the heather around its hooves.

"Elin!" I yell as his horse bolts, unresponsive to his commands.

This only ends in tragedy if I don't stop it.

Dropping the canteen to grab my reins, I kick my horse into a hard sprint, leaning forward and low, giving it its head.

A dark, familiar voice whispers in my ear. *"Meddling with fate, are we?"*

"Not here, not now," I hiss through gritted teeth. Only I can hear this voice. It belongs to the one I serve—the one who sent me to this country in the first place, saying there was someone I needed to meet, but was infuriatingly sparse on the details.

"What will be, will be."

"Please," I beg. "Not this way."

"All living things are mine to take. Or have you forgotten?"

Bitter tears leak from my eyes. Loss and grief are my constant companions, the question almost cruel. One doesn't serve Death for centuries, witnessing countless ends, and not keenly understand life's finality. "But you can't have this one."

Available in ebook and paperback.